The Eatington concept was created by
Todd & Daniel J. Barnes.

Story outline by Todd Barnes
Words by Sarah Barnes,
Art & story by Daniel J. Barnes.

For all you little Bananas out there that think you're not brave enough to chase your dreams.

You are.

BRAVE BANANA

by Todd, Sarah & Daniel J. Barnes

On the edge of a town called Eatington,
A banana tree stands proudly.
Over crowded by a growing bunch,
But only one is sleeping soundly.

A Bunch of bananas hang high up in a tree,
But a few were plotting to be mean.
For one banana was a little different from the rest,
He was far more yellow than green.

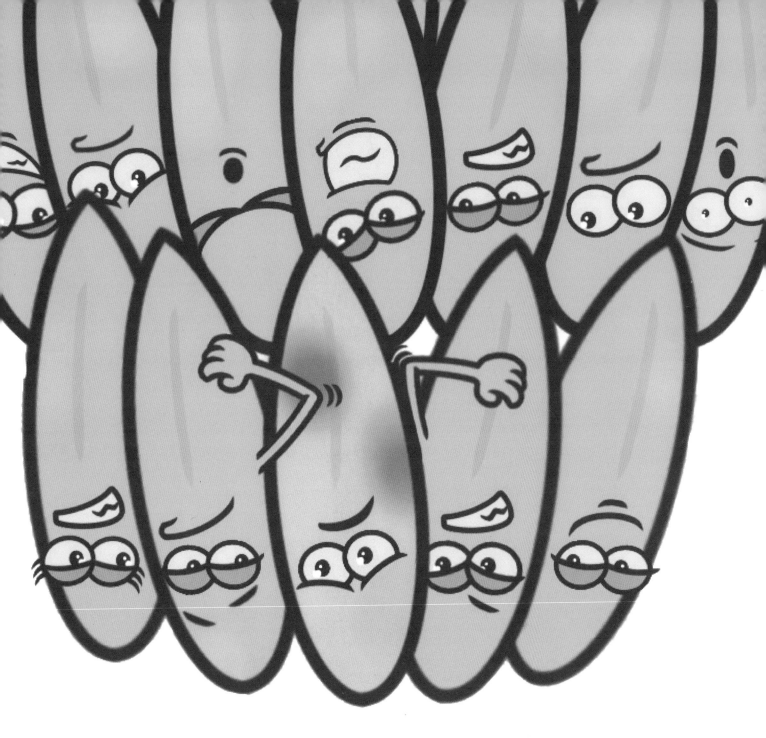

The others started to push him out,
And he fell quickly to the floor.
The bruised banana crying, stood up,
And put a plaster on his sore.

The bruised Banana walks on for a while,
Feeling sad and alone.
He comes across a little town,
A place to possibly call home.

He stumbles across an Emotional Egg,
And simply cannot just walk away.
A need to help him takes control,
A feeling that makes him stay.

Emotional Egg lays next to a wall,
With a crack in the top of his head.
Banana quickly removes his plaster,
And puts it on the poor fellow instead.

Emotional Egg is so happy,
And gets back on his feet without delay.
Banana feels so proud of himself,
He smiles as he walks on his way.

Everything is not what it appears today,
Because the Greedy Grape Gang are back in town.
As always, this sour bunch is up to no good,
Their antics bringing everyone down.

21

They're heading towards Mr Banger's shop,
Where he sells chicken, pork and bacon.
Banana watches in surprise,
As a link of sausages are taken.

GULP!

Banana wants to stop them,
So stands tall to block their path.
But the gang aren't too happy,
And prepare to unleash their wrath.

PC Nut is on hand to foil the deed,
By grabbing hold of a link.
He knows just what they need,
A night spent in the clink.

No free meal for the Grapes today,
And the Greedy Grape Gang look ashamed.
As the constable leads them away,
The naughty scoundrels tamed.

Mr Banger couldn't be happier,
Why, he's as pleased as punch.
He thanks Banana for his courage,
And for foiling that naughty bunch.

There's a fire up the street,
Chip's Chip Shop is ablaze!
The Chip family are lost and frantic,
Unable to see through the smokey haze.

The fire brigade are on their way,
Ready to tackle the fire.
With hose at the ready and ladder in hand,
They're here to tackle that flaming fryer.

The S'mores arrive on the scene,
And surely they can help.
But as they near the fire, catastrophe!
They all begin to melt!

A crowd has gathered with a feeling of dread,
As they watch on consumed with fear.
Can anybody help poor Baby Chip?
As the smoke and flames draw near.

Feeling brave, Banana starts to climb the ladder,
Making sure he doesn't slip.
He hears the crying through the smoke,
Can he save Baby Chip?

41

Baby Chip is stuck in the window,
Banana can hear her sad tears.
He manages to reach in and grab her,
To the sound of overwhelming cheers.

Banana proudly hands back Baby Chip,
Mr and Mrs Chip are ever so glad.
Banana has been so brave,
Oh, what a day he's had.

Everyone has heard of Banana's big day,
A parade is being held by the Mayor.
He wants to give Banana a reward,
A moment for all of Eatington to share.

Mayor Walter Melon presents Banana with a sticker,
He's shown kindness in every way.
As Banana blushes with pride, the Mayor shouts,
"Brave Banana has saved the day!"

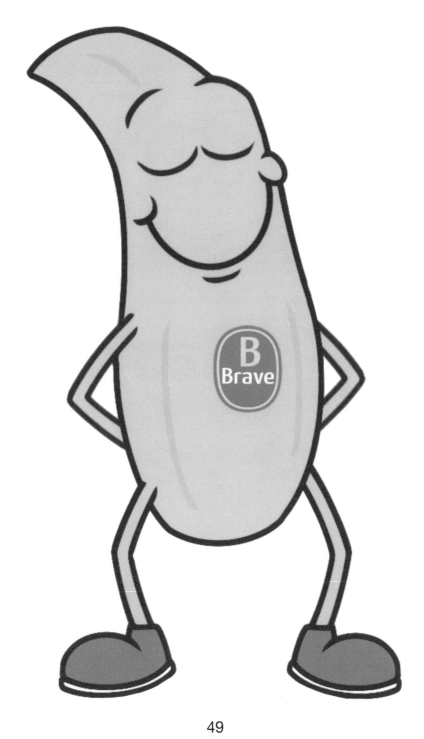

Thank you for reading.

Sarah, Todd & Daniel J. Barnes

Printed in Great Britain
by Amazon

30660843R10030